Fading American Farm

Nathanael Stump

PublishAmerica
Baltimore

© 2010 by Nathanael Stump.
All rights reserved. No part of this book may be reproduced, stored in a retrieval system or transmitted in any form or by any means without the prior written permission of the publishers, except by a reviewer who may quote brief passages in a review to be printed in a newspaper, magazine or journal.

First printing

All characters in this book are fictitious, and any resemblance to real persons, living or dead, is coincidental.

PublishAmerica has allowed this work to remain exactly as the author intended, verbatim, without editorial input.

Hardcover 978-1-4512-9422-4
Softcover 978-1-4512-9423-1
PUBLISHED BY PUBLISHAMERICA, LLLP
www.publishamerica.com
Baltimore

Printed in the United States of America

Contents

Perennial Memories 7
Grandpa's Ridge 9
Groundhog Wars 11
Croquet Creativity 14
APB on Uncle Buster 17
Highballers and Skin 20
Uncle Flip 23
Red Bull vs. Brown Dog 27
BB Guns and Black Birds 30
My First Buck 32
Sledding in High Socks 35
The Christmas Tree Tractor 38
The Antenna Star 40
Heading into Town 42
Hospital Visits and Kit Kats 46
Neighbors like Bummy 50
The Farm Pond 53
The Burning Barrel 55

These family and farm life stories are based on true life events with memories that will never fade. Thank you to Grandma Stump for taking time to reminisce life out loud with me, my Dad, for correcting the details of her exaggerated stories and my children, for giving me a reason to write them down.

Perennial Memories

When they moved to the farm in 1954 and bought seventy five acres for $11,000 the landscaping had not sold Grandma's spirits. Her plot was drabby and a bit dead. She went right to work, making the most of at hand materials beginning with a rock garden off the back porch. She filled the small beds beside the milk house cooler with day lilies, peonies, azaleas, and delphinium. She found starters of lilac, forsythia and rose of sharon from her mother's house in town and transplanted them with a fussy prayer. White summer snow bushes of spiraea bloomed every June along the black cracked driveway. Hyacinths were her trophies. The cone magenta flowers sprung up in surprising places, dripping their fragrant perfume around her porch.

She stood on the steps and instructed Grandpa on where to shovel spots for rose of sharon bushes on the right side of the farm lane. He dulled his shovel and his romance locating the perfect site, just to hear of another six inches down the hill. She had her order to the yard-art that no one else could see. Grandma was meticulous about where the empty pots should be stacked—under the porch or in the cellar corner for those that just might make it next year. She had to have the hose pressure sprinkly for annuals and full blast potential for black snakes climbing up the bird feeders. Her swan pots had to sit "Just so," and the sun porch plants each had their assigned seat while outside. Grandma did not practice crop rotation with her spring planting.

"It was right there last year, and yes it was a red one."

Grandma didn't believe in redoing a room, a flower bed or weed for that matter.

Her hickory-dickory-dock display of plastic animals was scattered everywhere around the farmhouse. The 50 lb raccoon had to be repainted every two years so Grandma could see those purple grapes he was snatching. The frog with the bikini sat under an umbrella that broke off because of, "That obnoxious little Eric and his ball games." The cow with the hose-spraying tail needed to graze into anorexia in the same dried out spot. Her wooden swing boys and girls that Grandpa jig-sawed floated from the catalpa tree. The white duck with her three and a half little peeps (half due to a weed whacking incident Grandma never forgot) rounded the begonia bush.

Down in the cellar window Grandma had a crown of thorns bush she received the year my Uncle Buster, the eldest was born. It poked me each time I'd go down to get her pots. The bush was approaching seventy the last year I was her maintenance man. It looked like it could have been the original from Israel. But I was "dare'cnt" to move it for the fear of her wrath, let alone God's. It was sacred to her just like all the other shriveled up greenery wilting on the basement window sill.

What really mattered to Grandma were her hanging baskets. One from my Uncle Buster on Mother's Day, Dinee on her yearly visit to Mifflintown, and two or three hung by Aunt Mary Kay the day after she arrived from Tennessee and wandered across town to the "expensive" greenhouse. Grandma adored a good fountain of petunias or the fallen pedals of bleeding hearts on her outdoor carpeted floor. They deserved the special watering can with just a touch of miracle grow juice from the dollar store. I'd watch her make the rounds to each floating bowl, hobbling over with a cane and a plastic green water pitcher. She made such a fuss over them you'd think they were her real children (ones that listened anyway). Grandma would sweet talk them into pollinating. Her lips would move gently over each pot with a prayer of simple blessing.

Every flower reminded Grandma of something so picture-perfect in life. Perhaps the time she sat out in the garden and Grandpa snapped a Polaroid of her in the tulips, then kissed her on the cheek. Maybe a memory of her glory, bringing her darling Mary Kay up the porch steps for the first time. The olfactory sense she breathed in helped her reminisce the wedding of her first grandchild. Grandma saw geraniums and shed a tear over her mother's grave. And oh, this one here took her back to an Easter morning when she stood up in her son, Charlie's, little country church to accept Jesus and the crown he bore for her eternal beauty.

Grandpa's Ridge

West on Route 322, Pennsylvania, right after the railroad tracks along the river, I'd start squirming out of my car seat. Three hours and twenty two minutes in, I'd be asking my parents nonstop questions.

"Are we there yet? Can I see his mountain too?" When I saw the reproduction statue of liberty pointing in the Susquehanna River I knew we were getting close.

"Which mountain is it Daddy?"

"Around the next corner Nathanael, now get back in your seat and crack your window for the dog!" My dad, Charlie, had a insatiable taste for used cars. Like his father, Dad drove full-size cars with way back seats that only got fifteen miles a gallon and were traded in before every birthday because they smoked too much. But there was plenty of room for a family of six and their Australian Sheppard to make a weekend trip to the farm. Our dog Joy, rode along if we were going to the 'country' grandparents, and not the 'city ones'. Grandpa and Grandma's farm was postcard perfect, nestled in the foothills of boyhood freedom.

"Is that Grandpa's ridge, Dad? The blue one, right?" I couldn't believe my Grandpa Stump had a whole mountain named after him. He must have been someone special for sure. I mean to have his own mountain you could see from the highway must have made him famous. Only astronauts and explorers had their own mountain. Grandpa's Ridge was legendary to me. I tried to follow Dad's finger with my blue eyeball and got dizzy. Though I lost the spot in the purple blend of the rolling hills, I always said I saw it. The blue one, Grandpa's Ridge, my Grandpa's Ridge!

As soon as my family could see the farm's ridge top, we'd play the "Guess Grandma's Lunch Game." All six of us had one guess as to what Grandma's Pennsylvania Dutch Dish would be that day. I declared outright, lunch would be my favorite, hotdogs with warm buns and beefaroni. Mom said we'd be dining around the extended table leafs on vegetable soup and homemade rolls. Dad went adult on us.

Looking at me in the rearview mirror he said with exaggeration, "Roast beef, mashed potatoes, and dark dirty brown gravy!"

"Gross'ning," I said, as I leaned out the window. I saw that blue ridge and could taste Grandma's homemade sweet seeped tea. I'd watched her as I sat on the ripped orange vinyl padded chair in the kitchen and learned perfection required six teabags and three long squirts from the toy lemon in the refrigerator. I can still smell the warm rolls under the napkin in the basket. I'd steal a Hartley's chip from the plastic bowl when she was setting the table.

As we rolled off the Mifflintown exit I pictured Grandpa as king of the mountain. I knew he was up on the hills of the farm waiting impatiently for me to arrive. He was probably climbing up a hemlock tree on the highest point of the ridge looking for me. Yep, Grandpa would be scouting for our bubbly blue woody wagon coming up his lane, listening for the popping of stone pebbles announcing his favorite Grandson was coming. I saw his cigarette smoke in the clouds and his bic lighter in the late morning sun.

Turning right off route 35 at the Citgo station, Dad argued, the mountain didn't have a name, but I was sure "Grandpa's Ridge" was on the map. After all, I heard everybody talk about it on the porch as I played underneath the wooden slats. Years later when I could finally read a map, I found Forge Hill on the topographic. Made me wonder as a boy and now as a grown up kid, what would I name a mountain given the rights? Now that's something to talk about over lunch. I think I'd call my mountain, Grandpa's Ridge!

Groundhog Wars

The heat of summer sizzling over the garden brought the old groundhog out of hiding. It had a hole under the toolhouse and crept guardedly towards the organic appetizers. He'd stop to scratch an itchy back on the rusty wire tomato stakes. Layers of thick skin and rolling fat brushed passed big boy tomato stalks, onion sets and carrot tops. The smell of romaine lettuce could always get his nose twitching. And if the shiny metal monster was missing from under the shade tree, or the lawn chair sat vacant under the wind chimes, that fat little critter would make a mad dash at the buffet.

Grandpa Stump left his gun out back, leaning by the screen door latch. The old .22 propped against the brick wall all summer long begged any boy to touch her. His big Mossburg 12 gauge was right inside the kitchen door beside his rubber galoshes. He was convinced something was going through his garden like a starving vegetarian in a produce aisle. Grandpa bought a box of shells down at the hardware store just in case. He told Grandma it was most likely a woodchuck. If Grandpa's farm defending, gut instincts were correct, war was eminent. Man against beast, Woodchuck verse Stump.

Grandpa would sit on the back porch for hours, barely breathing in anticipation of the garden beast. He attempted to camouflage himself by wearing a red flannel short sleeve shirt. His body vaguely blended in with the fake brick veneer. But every time Grandpa lost patience and made a run for the kitchen to grab a pack of peanut butter crackers, the beast struck. That wise old woodchuck rushed in and took out a cabbage plant.

"Well how about you, boy," he would say, and spit over the porch railing.

It became the five o'clock conversation over fried chicken and potato pancakes. He told Grandma they'd be eating fried groundhog thighs soon.

"Bet they use groundhog meat at the 322 Diner," she responded.

Grandpa had purchased the groundhog gun at an estate auction. It was a bolt action he had bore sited by his neighbor, Bummy. Fine tuned, it still played like a corroded, cracked clarinet blown by a fourth grader. It shot every other bullet. You had to make do for wind gusts stronger than a summer breeze. He tested the rifle's accuracy on pill bottles, Raid cans and milk jugs full of water. The milk jug didn't bare many leaks to say the least. He'd throw the gun-site out of kilter by breathing so heavy in a rage when he caught a glimpse of the four-legged, lettuce-eating beast.

Grandma would come out on the porch to defend the underdog living under her shed. This was Stump's own World War III right on her front porch, and she did not care for Grandpa's hostility in the least. She thought the critter was kind of cute and maybe they could just take him as a p.o.w. Grandpa would not tolerate her argument for a second.

"No one traps groundhogs," he said. "Ya just shoot 'em! Whoever heard of a pet groundhog anyway. They just lay around and nibble on your home grown food all day." Grandma wanted to know what the difference was between Grandpa and the varmint.

"Sounds a lot like you, Stump, and you don't see me baring down on you with some old rifle, do you?"

Grandpa reminded her of what a prize country tomato plant would look like with teeth marks punctured all through the red skin. He informed her that the entire garden could possibly cave in one day with the chuck's underground network of trenches. On lazy afternoons he would daydream about the insurance he could collect if this would indeed happen. His oldest son worked up at the insurance office in town and taught him about deductibles.

He was basking in his millions when the sound of a woodchuck call echoed through his hearing aid. Grandma said there was no such thing as a groundhog signal but Grandpa had bought a plastic call at Wal-mart for $6.99, on clearance. He kept it in his 'miscellaneous' drawer down in the basement with other 'just in case' items still in the package. It made him feel better to know someone might ask to borrow it one day and Grandpa could say, "No!"

With military precision Grandpa swiveled the old gun up to his shoulder. He carefully propped the muzzle down on top of the geranium planter. He pretended to drown Grandma out in concentration as she yakked over potting mix on the outdoor carpet. Grandma raised a tiff threatening she'd clap and give the groundhog fair warning. The silver bead of that .22 shimmered like a diamond in those red pedals. Dirt started erupting from the pot as Grandpa twitched a bit. He was eying up the fat rodent in his crosshairs.

The live target was chomping on a leaf of lettuce, not making eye contact with the furious farmer. The obese animal was snickering at him, enticing him to pull the trigger. Grandpa's pointer finger danced like a leaf in a thunderstorm. Across the porch, Grandma heard the click of the safety and covered her ears. Bang!

Birds came darting out of the nearest dwelling on a pole. Grandpa would now have to do a little rehab on the birdhouse, out in his own toolhouse. The groundhog bolted for the wire fence before Grandpa slipped in the third shell. Grandma laughed till her sides hurt at the predicament. Every time he told the story, Grandpa claimed he'd just fired a warning shot!

Croquet Creativity

Whichever farm boy finished his chores first, was given access to the rack of croquet mallets and multi-colored balls. Little Charlie, who always finished in second place was colorblind and thought the red balls were actually green. Typically boys did not choose red as first pick. But Charlie colored his trees with red crayons in the first grade and kids called him crazy. He considered himself a romantic. I'm sure the grass was spotted with red blood now and then from the brothers' competitive nature. The hillside created a challenging fairway for big brother Buster to craft the ultimate course and maintain bragging rights of Mifflin Hill.

Buster, always taking charge, measured out the hoop distances with a contractor's tape and laid out the obstacles with a snicker. He drug out a copper gutter for a bridge, a horizontal milk-can for an end stake, and designed the long shot up the barn ramp with a fake groundhog hole or two. He dug the booby traps in with a couple maul like swings from the mallet. Buster made it securely impossible for his little brother Charlie to gain much of a lead. Ordered to freshen up the lanes, Charlie stomped behind the reel mower and buzzed the grass to golf course green perfection. Grandma was concerned it would leave a burned out, parched look. Buster cooled her worries down by walking up to the metal screen window, ensuring his mother Charlie would water the fairway with a hose when the game was over

Buster shot Chinese style through the legs instead of the classic side swing, which allowed for accuracy and precision when weaving through routes in the front yard. Charlie copied this style and still uses it in his sixties, reminiscent of a Tiger Woods with hemorrhoids stance. The arguments stemmed over things like cowpies interfering with rolling momentum.

Buster said, "If the dog carries the ball closer to the hoop, then, so be it!"

There was an unwritten rule that send-offs were for beginners. So they chose to take an advantage shot when bumping colors. Charlie was the king of double hoops but Buster could hit the long ball and fly right by, leaving his little brother breathless.

The boys played under car lights and even fire flies. Their father, my Grandpa Stump, thought the game was for girls, but still watched from the porch. Grandpa did take notice of the game enough to place cigarette bets on the winner with "Little Grandpa" his wife's father.

One July post supper was proclaimed the Mifflintown Tourny-Men. Little sister, Mary Kay, adorned in all white, including matching ribbons in her long dark hair, refereed when she wasn't fixing her hair. Neighbor Jeffery Potter took the blue ball and "Lightning" Larry Wise went with orange. Buster's best friend, Dusty, chose the black ball, which left the brothers with green and red.

The chase was tight even down through the garden gate and up the concrete slabs past the milkhouse shack. The pack stayed close to each other's P.F. Flyer sneakers, down the bank to the mailbox. Buster shot a screamer up the lane and bounced it off the white ring leaving it vibrating with everyone's envy. He lit a cigarette and turned to receive a blow-kiss from his girlfriend, lounging on the freshly mown grass. He said it counted for an extra shot since it technically went 60% through the wire rim and reversed its way back to the entrance of the tunnel. This led to a serious debate from Jeff who felt the ball never crossed the plane. After all, he was the closest, trying to sneak a peak at Buster's gal's long legs from behind her on the hill. They were about to throw down when Charlie walked right up to the green ball and whacked it down through two hoops in a row and hit the milk can.

He had missed the whole hoopla while double checking the roster card with his little sister. All the boys paused in silence and stood staring at the kid with the cowlick who had just masterfully shot the wrong ball down the final runway.

"That was my ball," said Buster with a clenched fist.

"Looked red to me," said Charlie. "Almost as red as your face, Johnny!" No one called him Johnny.

Buster ran full bore at his little brother. He was coming like a locomotive with cigarette smoke steaming from his nostrils. The hand made mallet hole he had made caught his P.F.'s by complete surprise. The wooden hammer went airborne and Buster slid home-plate style straight into a moist cow bomb with a crusty pudding exterior. The boys laughed till they soaked their drawers, while running a safe distance from the smeared victim. Little Grandpa reached back over to reclaim a cigarette from his son in law.

With a wheeze of a laugh, he declared, "I say we call it a draw!"

APB on Uncle Buster

Buster first saw Sandy at a Mifflintown softball game. He was catcher and she caught his eye in the bleachers at three o'clock high. He missed an easy lob ball that hit him in the waist line while staring at her short shorts. After the game, Buster was drinking a yuengling with some friends on the tailgate of his yellow Chevy truck. Sandy paraded by wearing a tight spaghetti strap shirt and those blue shorts showing skin season was in. Buster let out a sharp whistle. A week later, when his friend Dick set him up on a blind date in Lewistown, the same summer girl with the spaghetti strap shirt walked in the Italian restaurant. Buster nearly fell out of his chair.

Sandy was a catholic girl who attended Sacred Heart Parish every Saturday evening with her strict Italian family. Buster would wait for her outside the IGA supermarket down the street, and they would take off for the riverbank, the drive in theatre or just go for a drive. Her daddy was a deputy sheriff so they had to cruise on back roads instead of parading down town in his yellow chevy truck laying rubber like the other teenagers. Sherriff Dilissio did not like the idea of a protestant farm boy from Juniata being in his backyard, back-pew, or backseat to say the least. Sandy's mom excommunicated them from each other after finding Buster's team pennant in her daughter's backpack.

However, Buster was the kind of boy that would get his way no matter what anyone said. He drove around town in the back of a pick up shooting cats with a .22, roaring at the driver about which alleys to take. Buster stayed out late and skipped Sunday School for the freshly mown Juniata park ball fields while his little brother and sister sat perfectly still in the pew beside their Grandmother. He ordered his little brother Charlie to make cigarette runs while he and Grandpa worked on the outbuildings. Buster demanded Charlie wheelbarrow the manure up the ramp as a daily chore. They had an argument one day over who would do manure and who would milk. Buster said he could do both faster than Charlie could eat a Clark bar. Little Charlie was sitting on a milk can watching, when Buster fell off the edge of the ramp into the manure spreader and the caked brown wheelbarrow landed on top of his head. Charlie had to shovel out the manure ditches for a month because he chuckled while taking a sniff of Buster's shirt collar.

So when Buster was told by the Dilissio family to stay away, their commandment made him pursue Sandy all the more. He came up with a scheme to elope, but knowing he was dealing with a small town sheriff, he brought his farm family in on the getaway.

They parked Buster's Chevrolet truck in the barn and covered it with hay. He tossed Grandpa's car keys in the air as he walked down the farm lane in the crisp October evening. The silo was full of feed corn, the alfalfa was cut, the cows were milked for the night and the woman of his dreams was primping in front of a mirror, preparing to cut and run to Georgia. Everyone knew you could go there and get hitched without a waiting period. He made plans to drive non-stop south, get married and make a life of it back at the farm when things simmered down. He fired up his dad's Bel Air, honked twice at the porch light and turned left to head into the town rendezvous.

The sheriff banged on the door at 11:53 pm. Grandpa looked over at Grandma and took another spoonful of home-made ice-cream.

"It's about that time," he said.

The knocking grew louder as Grandpa slowly strolled across the kitchen linoleum and stopped at the fridge to pour a glass of milk. Grandma stayed in her green chair watching television, pretending not to be vexed. The knocking kept up with a steady non-stop rhythm now. Grandpa opened the green door and was eye to eye with sheriff Dilissio through a single pain of glass.

"Where are they Stump?"

"Where's who?" said Grandpa, as he took a sip of cold milk from his white stained glass.

"That stupid big boy of yours and my daughter. We haven't seen her since mass let out!"

"Oh well Buster, he's not much of a church boy you know. He went up turkey hunting with Ed."

"Like hell he did! Hen hunting hugh? You know I'll find them don't you?" Grandma strolled out to the kitchen pretending to be rounding up some ice cream dishes.

"Why sheriff Dilissio, I haven't seen you in a coon's age. How's that pretty girl of yours? Sandra is it?"

The sheriff slammed the door and walked out on the back porch to make a radio call. He ordered an all points bulletin for a 1948 yellow Chevy pick up truck. Stump came out the kitchen door and shut it tightly behind him. He glanced over at the barn where the sheriff had parked in the turnaround and then caught Dilissio's eye.

"Tell them it's an *advance design series* and I think there's a couple bails of hay in the bed. You'll probably see a whole trail of hay heading north."

The sheriff stormed off mad, cursing under his breath. As he flipped on his red and blue lights heading down the farm lane, Grandpa hoisted his glass of fresh milk and cheered his son's prosperity.

When Buster and Sandy Stump returned up the farm lane honking a week later, Grandma was on the porch smiling and thinking about grandbabies. They brought in a mobile home and parked it just beyond the garden. The sheriff tapped his brake lights driving down Licking Creek Road when he saw the tractor pulling the trailer across the lane, but refused to stop in and see Sandy for three years. Buster and Grandpa decided to build modular homes together on the hillside across the road. The grand finale of *Stump Development*, as the locals call it, was a white ranch placed on a poured slab. Buster said basements were a thing of the past but had to expand with a family room when he and Sandy had their fourth: twins, one boy, one girl.

Sandy's parents lifted the excommunication when grandchildren came into the picture and melted hard hearts. Buster and Sandy had their 50th wedding anniversary Oct 24th 2009, at the fire hall right across from the courthouse where her daddy's station used to be. The twins put the whole celebration together and big brother Bob, a protestant reverend, had his parents say their vows on northern soil. Sandy cried like an old lady at mass. Buster, looking like a spitting image of Grandpa Stump, suspenders, hiked up pants and slicked back grey hair, gave the ladies in the receiving line extra long hugs and talked to me about heading up to hunting camp.

Highballers and Skin

The farm family had a secret fascination with the city life. Grandpa and Grandma used to live in town by the river when they first got married. Grandma said they'd go to the theatre on Saturday nights and Grandpa would stare at the skin on the screen with a smile. She slapped him now and then and said he just wanted to watch the legs and nothing else.

"You could of stayed home and stared at chicken for free," she'd say. "All the skin and legs you want." He'd stare hard at her and store up revenge for later.

Sometimes they would go into the American Legion and order highballers, scotch whiskey and carbonated water. After several of these, Grandma sat on her stool and watched Grandpa attempt something that resembled a mating dance. He more or less gyrated his head around and shook his shoulders. She shook her head and turned back to the conversation with her cousin about the boy who came to the farm and took 51 cats for experimental reasons. Grandma hoped her lack of eye contact would keep Grandpa from embarrassing himself on the parquet floor.

The farmer and his wife even went to State College with Buster and Sandy a few times for a really big time. They would sit at a round table together and order whisky sours. The road trips ended when Aunt Sandy got a bloody nose from Buster going one on one with a river bank. But the wild nights carried on. Buster's adventurous daughter, Debbie, smacked her car into the neighbor's brick wall one alley way away from home on a Saturday night. She was singing with the radio, making her way back home from a party. The rookie deputy sheriff let her go because she was so beautiful.

Occasionally the lane would be full of cars on a Saturday night at the farm house. Grandpa and Grandma hosted parties now and then for friends and family. My dad, Charlie, who was supposed to stay up stairs with his radio, told me there was music, drink, and more cigarette smoke than Three Mile Island produced. The TV would be blaring with Ed Sullivan's showcase and the davenport, Grandma's name for the formal couch, actually had someone sitting in it. The scarlet red seat with the plastic covering was only taken after a couple home-made highballers.

I guess the social get togethers could get pretty roaring. Charlie would sneak down the stairs after listening through the floor vents. When all the guests had gone, the boy hid behind the crack in the door, comforted by the feel of his mother's fur coat hanging on the hook, and waited for the worst. Now and then Grandpa would get really fired up at something sarcastic Grandma had said and slap her around. She never even hinted at this in all the hush-hush conversations I had with her at the farm house. But my father, Charlie, cried in front of me, looking back on his family life one night from his own kitchen table. I think its only one of two times I've seen him sob. Alcohol, smoking, and the celebrity lifestyle take a reality check when you watch your dad crying like a little kid again. Seeing his mother's skin break and bleed must be the reason he never drank a drop or smoked a drag.

My dad, Charlie, chose to pursue other passions in life. Little Grandpa thought Charlie would go all the way with his DJ career. At age sixteen, Charlie was the host of his own radio show in little Mexico, Pennsylvania, that is. Little Grandpa would sit in his rocker in the corner of the farm house dining room and fall asleep listening to Charlie spin new sounds. I ran into Jim, the local well driller, at the Mifflintown Barber Shop. He told me my father Charlie was "electric" when he ran "Royal Bandstand" at the community fire hall. They gave Charlie forty dollars from the cover charge and the night was filled with the great Rock sounds of the sixties. Dad even moved up to working at the station in the big city of Lewistown during college and collected quite a few 45's under the entertainer name, "Chuck Lawrence".

Grandpa and Grandma thought Chuck might just go all the way, until he told them he was going to be the Summer Chaplain at RB Winter State Park. Charles chose to entertain people at an outdoor chapel on Sunday mornings, instead of the Saturday night disc jockey thing. Grandpa said he'd never make enough money to live on and didn't understand the career leap. Evidently Charlie had his radio on, up in his farm house bedroom one night while his parents partied down below. He got saved listening to the powerful booming voice of evangelist, Billy Graham preaching, "By His stripes we are healed." He actually became a minister who loves preaching and has a passion for people. He made pulpits and porch visits his living for over 40 years. Charlie's last church position before he retired was in Mifflintown, where he accompanied his Grandma every Sunday growing up.

Uncle Flip

Aunt Mary Kay was a bit of a southern belle from the start. She was tall and skinny, a pretty gal from Mifflin Hill who hated the thought of getting eggs from the chicken house. Egg gathering did not match her feminine mystique. She was more of a doll baby outfit designer, hair brusher, bath taker and chore watcher, not a doer. She shared a pink wallpapered room with Grandma till she was actually of college age and was compelled to move to a dorm room on her campus. She loved long silky baths in the claw tub, fluffy kittens, elegant flowers, and fine china. She anticipated setting the table with trinkets and accessories to match the day of the week or an approaching holiday. She was a little spoiled, the only girl after two boys, and fifteen years younger than the oldest. She was Grandma's pet project as much as Buster, the oldest, was Grandpa's construction specialist.

So when Miss Mary Kay, the teacher from Green Park Elementary School, told her mom and dad she was taking a cruise with a college friend, the family was perturbed to say the least. Grandpa felt cruises were for the upper class and not farm girls from Pennsylvania. He said she could buy a car from Leighty Cheverolet for the same damn price as a one week cruise to the Caribbean. Grandma required a post card from every port with constant reports and check ins. Secretly in her own heart, Grandma wanted to go, but didn't even have her driver's license, let alone think about taking up a seat by an airplane window. Sometimes she lived vicariously through her daughter's travels and future trips. But no one, in their wildest imagination could have had any idea of the 'momento' Mary Kay would be bringing home from her cruise.

He was a six foot four blonde boy from Holland working as an engineer in the generator room of the cruise ship. Grandma called him Sunny Boy. We called him Uncle Flip. They called him over to budge a bolt, reimagine the broken, and repair the unthinkable. He drank Heineken half and half with Guinness, drove a motorcycle to the dock and just left it there, and once was arrested for smashing a gum ball machine that cheated him out of his hard earned cash. He had pearly teeth his father paid big bucks to perfect. Flip's father was an oil rig captain who had him sporadically live with different relatives after his mother passed away when Flip was eight. His hair was feathered, with distracting clothes that covered up the grease-marks as he ventured on deck under star lit skies to case out those young female passengers. He and his buddy inspected the American girls with curiosity and cockiness.

When he saw all 6 feet 1 inch of Mary Kay, he just wanted to pinch her. Flip knew what he wanted and went for it. But after some giggling, she crafted a deal that there would be no date unless Flip could find someone for her best friend. He turned right around, marched over to his buddy and the four of them were at a private table that very night. And, guess what? Both couples climaxed their romantic journey at an American Church altar.

Flip asked Mary Kay to marry him down by the bridge just a half mile from Grandpa's farmstead. He almost waited to propose at the picturesque place where the stream wound its way under a rustic wooden bridge. It was a rural paradise with huge hovering limbs of hundred-year old shade trees, offering pastoral serenity to a spot he chose for his kneeling petition.

But Flip was actually quite nervous from Little Grandpa yelling to Mary Kay's father, "Are you going to let her marry that damn foreigner!"

Given the threat in the air, Flip hastily stopped by a washed out trench on the gravel road en route to the originally planned site and proposed right there. He wanted her to say yes before his future father in law figured out what he had really asked permission for with his Dutch accent.

The permission to marry Mary Kay went over as well as the first time Flip asked to drive the tractor. Grandpa was cautious to say yes and knew his suspicions were correct when he watched Flip leap off the tractor barefoot while it barreled down the hill. Grandpa watched that tell-tale incident from his porch shaking his head in dismay. But by then he had an American girl about to be shown the world who had fallen into Flip's brawny arms and met his baby skin smile with a kiss.

FADING AMERICAN FARM

They first moved to Erie but after having Phil and then a second son named Eric they bought a house just two properties over from Grandpa's farm. Flip liked to be on the go, in the hunt for big money, along with fancy hotel rooms and fine meals. He thrilled on driving fast shiny cars and, at the same time, listening to audio books on the Civil War. Mary Kay loved her living room and short jaunts to her mother's kitchen. In the 70's Flip was offered a $50,000 salary to be a supervisor for a big generator company. But Uncle Flip was an entrepreneur from the time he attempted making money with his own snack shop at age ten. This boy who was born on an island was destined to be one of a kind.

Uncle Flip decided to make money on his own instead of the $50,000 company job. He sent letters to hospitals all over America looking to upgrade generators. After working on them in tight spaces in ocean liners, he knew he could rig them out of basements, roll them on metal casters, load them on double drop trailers by crane, and then sell them to professional scrappies all around the country. He hit the road more and more, found factory leftovers to sell and met the right circle of scrappers who knew the secret of those copper lines running all around plants and backtied into the very generators he was heaving out. It became a contemporary underground gold rush. He paid temp workers an extra twenty dollar cash bonus per day, bought their lunch and made the top two list of temp businesses to work for in California. Occasionally he'd run a beautiful truck off the berm and once severely burned his face and fingers on a high voltage mcm line, but always came out on top. With Golden hair and that baby skin, he looks more handsome today at 58 then most men in their 30's.

He told Uncle Buster how much he made in a year and Buster walked out of the farm house living room pouting. He chose Tennessee as a central location and moved Mary Kay to the South where her feminine mystique was quite at home. There the azaleas bloom by Easter and her Victorian house in St. Elmo could be the envy of any middle class Chattanooga neighborhood. They started taking annual trips to Europe, Chickatee Island, Holland, and of course, Grandpa and Grandma's farm six times a year.

Little Phil and Eric were the first boys I saw with an Atari video game system. They drove cool cars like their father's 65 mustang and took extended college tours. They wrecked those cars and bought replacements. They dated tall girls and tried to build their own world. Both returned to work for 'Pappa' in their own unique way, building the business, and continuing that hair raising reputation of their father. Flip's youngest, Adam, he called Peep, turned out to be the tallest and biggest hope for taking over River City Industrial. All three of Flip's boys still hit the road and send rigs of electrical equipment, copper and cash back to their dad's five warehouses.

Uncle Flip hired me to keep the farm standing and keep Grandma happy after her hip replacement. Uncle always paid me cash and a bonus for things that made Aunt Mary Kay smile when she came to visit. I worked for him one week in college and received enough money to buy my girlfriend an engagement ring. I worked for him two separate summers and watched him move men, sweet talk waitresses, close a big deal with a big wig, then eat lunch laughing with an ex prisoner temp worker. Grandpa and he sure butted heads now and again, but I'll never forget hearing how Uncle Flip went to visit him every night in the Lewistown hospital. Grandpa thanked him for the good things he'd done for the farm and asked him how much money he was making at his latest job.

"Wow," Grandpa responded, and fell asleep with an envious smile.

Red Bull vs. Brown Dog

We went to visit Grandma and Grandpa at the farm one April. Our dad had packed the push button fishing rods along with our dog, Joy, in the back of the station wagon. Mom had brought a Red Igloo cooler with A&P sodas and sandwiches which we gobbled down at the Midway exit. As soon as we pulled into the farm, Thaddeus and I dug up some worms and put them in an old coffee can. Sarah and Robin tried on their polka dot boots and matching rain jackets my mom picked up at the Round 2 consignment store back home. There was mud everywhere that time of year. Luckily our dog, Joy, was brown.

We had to duck under the electric fence to hike up to the pond. You could hear it ticking over at the tractor port. Joy ran right underneath and took off in front of our family pack of five. Mom stayed behind to make chocolate chip cookies and give Grandma a Toni Curl hair permanent. We passed the old metal cattle shed that was empty this morning. The cows were roaming the pasture somewhere out of sight. Grandpa was paid by a farmer down the road to let them graze in the Stump farm fields.

On the walk up to the pond Dad told us a story about fishing for sunnies at the Ericson's. He was there with my older sister one spring, when a mother goose felt Robin got too close for comfort and chased her spread eagle, honking like a Volkswagon. Dad had to ward the goose off with a Zebco Snoopy rod and fell in the water chasing the irate bird away from his little girl. We were all scared to death there'd be ducks or Canadian geese at the pond when we reached the bank. But Joy was already in the water scaring away the fish and every last living thing by the time we stepped onto the rocks at the edge of the farm pond.

I had Dad put a worm on my hook and started casting at the old metal drain pipe in the middle of the pond. My red and white bobber hit the water with a kerplunk and I reeled in my waterskiing worm at a swift pace.

Sarah immediately had her line caught in the pine tree and Robin was sitting on a rock reading a book on spiritual warfare. Dad was showing little Thad how to cast when the dog started growling. We turned around and Sarah started whimpering.

The bull was looking straight at us with his head down low. He was shaking his massive neck back and forth and his horns glimmered in the sun. Apparently bulls are annoyed by the color red and, therefore, quite irritated at my sister's slickers, our dad's hanky, my brother's Phillies hat, and my red Folger's can in my hand. The bull dragged a hoof across the slick mud and Dad whispered for us to all stay still and calm. The hair on the back of my dog Joy stood straight up as she eyed up the big brown bull, leading a group of ladies in tow for a cool drink of the same pool water we were fishing in. Dad started saying the "Our Father" out loud.

Sarah went from whimpering to hysterical before Dad got to, "...Who art in heaven." Robin who had just been reading *This Present Darkness* started rebuking the beast in the name of Jesus. Dad picked up Thad in his arms and stepped in front of all his children. I was backing into the water because I had never seen cows swim in the cowboy movies. I figured if I could get a head start and out swim my sisters I would avoid being trampled to death. Joy narrowed the gap between her scrawny self and the brute who had his eye on Sarah's red rain coat.

Our brown dog had a bit of Australian Shepherd in her genes and it was starting to rear itself. Her caramel eyes studied every twitch of the bull's drawn back ears. As the cow lowered his body to charge, Joy ran in at his feet. She must have made ten laps around him before he knew what had happened. My sisters were calling her back afraid she'd get a hoof to the head and Dad took the opportunity to take his children to higher ground. I dropped the worms in the water in disbelief as Joy started chasing the entire herd down over the bank and through the pasture field. Thad was crying, but Joy was in her glory getting those cows moving across the soft ground with particles of mud raining down behind the herd as they picked up speed. She stayed on their heels all the way to the cattle shed at the bottom of the pasture. She took her time returning to Dad's voice, the dog performing a spin around maneuver repeatedly to make sure the cows were not following behind.

When Joy made it back to the top of the hill, Dad said we'd have to give her a bath in the pond before heading down home. But as kids we did not care about dirt on a superhero dog. All four children ran to her, pulling our arms around that old brown girl. Joy sat facing south on the edge of the pond bank lavishing our pats and hugs. On the way back down to the farm Dad remembered the theory about red. He had us put a couple articles of clothing in his metal tackle box as we passed by the barn. I ran ahead to tell Grandma and Grandpa about our adventure with our brown dog Joy.

On the porch Grandpa cross-examined his son, Charlie, on the rule about red. But Dad blamed his color blindness on the innocent mistake, said it would make a great sermon illustration, Joy protecting Thy kingdom and keeping us from evil. Grandma gave the dog a heaping portion of beef stew in her bowl and a meat flavored milkbone for dessert.

BB Guns and Black Birds

Grandpa's farm was a walking war zone for bb gun bird hunts. There were enough potential targets on the farm for a daisy one pump to wear your little arm out. Grandpa had his own Red Ryder encased in the gun cabinet down in the basement. It was made of cherry wood with a god ugly curtain over the glass to keep little boys like me from thinking guns were really in there. I always liked to peek at them, wishing they were mine. I wondered who would get the guns if Grandpa ever died. I figured Uncle Buster would turn them in for cash. Aunt Mary Kay would burn them to ash. And my Dad would simply overlook them completely. I, however, I would hunt with them, just like Grandpa, but for bigger birds and wilder deer.

The farm was my training ground for the countdown to go deer hunting with Buster.

"Four more years," he'd say outside my car window as we prepared to pull down the lane to drive back to our house.

In preparation, milk jug caps became deer eyes. I loved watching them flip up and over into the air when I machine gunned them down with my gold ball blaster. The 2% milk cap would get a bigger A.P.R. when I was done with target practice. Chickadees became man-eating helicopters or Jap planes I took out in mid-air.

When I sat on the porch eying up the birdhouses, Grandpa urged, "Go get the blackbirds Nat. Your Grandma hates those damn blackbirds. They give her the Willie's."

I figured every bird had a little black on it somewhere to make all birds, in my mind, fair game. I never shot Robins, though. My oldest sister shared the same name and my Mom always made a huge fuss over the first one she'd see every spring. I let cardinals get free fly zones as well because they were crimson for sure and although easily spotted targets, not black. I must confess I fed a lot of cats with specified black birds.

FADING AMERICAN FARM

If it was up to me and my imagination, I would have just as soon shot cats for a living. I dreamt of being a professional feral cat hunter out in Wisconsin. I'd create a new hunting season killing off those critters that look like they are going to leap into your face and rip off your skin. When I was thirteen, I was at my friend Ian's house for dinner eating pizza, and his cat came at me airborne, fangs unleashed and claws unfurled. The wild cat left railroad marks on my skinny legs and took off with my pepperoni. I would have put a bb in every meow meow's butt from the farm to California if it wouldn't have been for all those interrogations I got from Grandma. She'd go F.B.I. on me when she saw mud on my skippies, as she called new sneakers. If she heard pellets in my pockets I was sure to get ten questions. She would shake her head and hold her hips praying out loud that I, "Dare'cnt hurt any cute birdies that the good Lord kept his eye on." You know, like the sparrow in that old church song.

"Only the black ones, Grandma," I said with a smirk. "Only the black ones!"

Years later I found myself installing new birdhouses at Grandpa's farm. Uncle Flip purchased them on a mini vacation to Maine with Aunt Mary Kay. They looked like rustic log cabins, and I even added caulking to the roofs to make them weather tight. Grandma made me put them up high so the blacksnakes could not wind their way up to the baby birdies in the summer. Placing each pole with concrete and bracing each little house with extra screws and brackets gave me an adult appreciation of her birds and their apartments. Hanging the houses from the Catalpa tree with its beanpod décor, I made sure to place the front door in Grandma's back porch view. I painted a stump on a white birdhouse Grandpa had left out in the workshop for repairs and hung it from the wagon shed peak. I even ended up placing two in my own backyard. My daughter and I clean them out each spring. She watches in fascination as we inspect the construction, curious how anything could live in a house as small as her head. She rides up with me on the red four-wheeler to place corn in the feeder and we pray out loud that we will be able to see deer and turkey(big birds as she calls them) from our sliding glass door.

My First Buck

I think Grandpa heard me yelling with exhilaration late that afternoon from up on his ridge. Somehow he always heard the echo of a rifle through those farmhouse walls. My seventeen year old screams of buck fever danced down the logging road, through the golden fields, poured down the spring stream and knocked three times on his green enameled front door. My father Charlie had not inherited Grandpa's hunting heart like Uncle Buster and I had. Grandpa and Buster ruled the ridge. They were rumored to have shot six deer at a time and have them hanging under the barn before lunch on the first day of the season. Dad took my brother Thaddeus a year before and missed a spike buck at fifteen yards out, but was pretty proud of the tree he nailed at twenty. Watching Dad one morning owl hoot his breath to see which way the wind was blowing over his open Bible pages inside his deer blind, my brother and I said the double sons must have been switched at birth. We played sports and built forts. Buster's boys read books, and hung the outdoors up on the hook.

I paced a hundred and two steps from the old turkey blind from which Grandpa would stalk these woods season after season. I placed my boot in his footprints. One bullet lay empty in the leaves, having executed the last breath of this magnificent forest beast. I shook like a little boy doing a stiffy in excitement over a cookie. In the illusiveness of the woods, the still form of the downed creature whispered me on.

I found him, yes, lying lifeless in the crayon colored leaves. One shot just like Grandpa coached me from the front porch. One shot to leave the others guessing. You either got so bored staring at leaves and were just checking to see if your gun really worked or just took the biggest buck that had ever been sighted in the cut corn fields surrounding Route 35. One shot was all a real hunter needed. The echo of that single shot still thundered through my ears and down the county line for every one else to spit at and lose hope. I'd just defied Uncle Buster's famous first morning quote. I'd always hear him saying it by 12 p.m. the first day of the season.

"Well, half the deer that are going to be shot are dead already!"

But Grandpa didn't spit on this late afternoon. He smiled and drooled while napping on the lay-z-boy chair.

I stood there calling for my dedicated hunting companions. But of course, they couldn't hear me hollering in the hollow from their remote locations. Dad was asleep on a sofa in Grandma's living room and my brother Thaddeus, out cold in the dining room rocking chair with the sheepskin seat. His rear-end was sitting in soft wool while I was out in the cold all day in Woolrich.

I warmed my hands in the blood of that buck. I thanked God out loud for the sacrifice of death that brings life, especially for our freezer. I took from his body like Grandpa impatiently taught Buster and Buster schooled me.

"Make sure to get rid of those damn scent sacks." First thing Grandpa would ask me about later. "Ruins the whole deer," he'd say. I touched each of the six points with a ceremony. I was one of them now, a Great White Hunter.

I'd heard Grandpa could take down two with one shot and have them both hanging in the barn within minutes. He was done gutting one before his cigarette was down to the filter. I'd seen with my own eyes rack after rack nailed to the tool shed ceiling. I dreamed of hunting with him in the days of herds of deer. So many deer you could hit one with the stock of your gun as it ran by. Grandpa could shoot one when he'd feel like it from his bucket-seat.

I pulled the buck by the horns down from the ridge all on my own. I wondered how Grandpa dragged a 150 plus pound deer by himself so many times before. I almost had a heart attack at seventeen. I swore I'd never smoke a secret cigarette to try to be like Grandpa again. Smoking was not as uncomplicated as those cowboys on horseback, or Grandpa driving a pick-up with a cigarette in his lips. They never show someone enjoying a smoke while dragging a dead carcass or hiking down a mountain.

Grandpa walked all the way out to the back garage port, emphysema and all.

"You got one what?" He sauntered out to the end of the porch, down the steps, up the lane, and past the wagon-shed to see his grandson's first buck. Usually, Grandpa had to pause three times and sit on a bucket just to reach the burning barrel. He forgot about his emphysema and almost jogged out to that six point. I pointed to the shadow on the ridge where the giant fell. He wanted to know exactly what time I shot. Bet he was tracing the boom he heard in his afternoon nap, while picturing one of those big boys.

"Your first buck on the ridge," he sang out loud. I was his grandson. I saw it in his eyes of pride and felt it in one of his rare pats to my back.

Sledding in High Socks

Grandma had one of those wooden Lightning Glider sleds hanging out on the workshop wall. Her grandsons took turns pulling the tethered rope up the hills and breaking records for long distance runs. I always wanted to take it up the logging road to the top of Grandpa's thirty acre ridge and ride down like an Olympic bobsledder. But that was too far of a hike for a ten year old with his inexperienced, six year old brother tagging along. Grandma wrapped Thad up like a special package being shipped FedEx from QVC. Thad wore his puffy blue snow suit, Grandma's scratchy scarf, and the bread bags she had saved for inside his moon boots. We'd get half way up the hill and he'd ask for a hitch-hike. I told him if he could jump on when I'd do a drive-by he was welcome to wait there and be a sloth, but he would miss out on the ride of his life. I sold him when I said he could be the first to tell our cousins how far we made it down the slope.

We perched the sled at the point of the hill, right where the Christmas trees grew. Beneath us was the little drain pond that froze over before the big pond above. I made my little brother check the solidity by walking on it on our way up. The ice would make a perfect runway and with both our weights, I figured we would really fly. Actually, we were trying to beat Grandma's record.

According to little Phil, Grandma and he had made the same exact trip three years prior. I couldn't believe she actually stepped off the porch. I never saw her walk further than the car waiting chauffer-style in the lane.

But on this rare snow day Grandma pulled up her high socks, strapped on her old taped up boots and said, "I'll race you to the top Sonny."

Of course they had to stop along the way to check out the neighbors and be snoopy. Grandma usually knew what was going on just from the views she could glimpse from her kitchen window. She showed Phillip how Ellen had the swing-door for her cats to march right into the garage and mess all over the place. She noted how Bummy had more cars than kids and how Gayle had no smoke coming out her chimney. She told little Phillip she expected Gayle's husband must have left her for good and now she had no one to carry in the wood. And she pointed up to Buster's house in Stump Development and said she could see that her son had shoveled out his own place but didn't bother to come salt her sidewalks.

They finally reached the peak where Grandma had to rest for a while. It was the perfect opportunity for little Phil to make some minor adjustments to the sled. He was destined to be an engineer and brought an adjustable wrench, a metal file and also a can of Pam that he commenced to spray on the bare metal while Grandma used her dainty hanker-chief. He made sure the blades were sharp to cut a trail and checked over each metal anchor like a human torque wrench. Grandma complained that she hadn't thought to bring a pillow for her arse and was worried about a splinter that could lead to hepatitis if unfound.

They both piled on the sled at the wood-line. This was the same starting line Uncle Flip had driven the runaway tractor down. Grandma placed her old worn boots in on the steering glide and little Phil snuggled in between to stay warm. The wind was starting to whip at them and shimmering snow was frosting their sleeves. She started to heave and ho so they could promptly get back to the warm farm house and boil some tea. It only took four thrusts and they were off with a giggle. The runners found a good groove and slid over the frozen ice topped with a dash of powder. Grandma was laughing so loud you would of thought her spleen would explode. Either that, or, far worse, she might wet her long underwear. Little Phil had to close his eyes but forgot to do the same with his mouth, screaming like an erratic little girl. The snow crystals piled up on his tongue like mounds of snow in a parking lot. Grandma just kept giggling dramatically reaching 28mph, the fastest she'd ever gone on snow or pavement.

When it was all over they were in the little overflow creek far below the pond and down by the burning barrel. They looked back at the two hundred yards they had covered in a couple seconds and burst into laughter.

"My lands," she said. "If it wasn't for this stream we could of made it all the way to the gas station for a gallon of milk."

Now back to this new moment of history. Thad and I knew we had to get over the pond, down the creek, and past that barrel as far as we could see in the falling snow. I told him I would push him like a bobsled crew and jump on top at the last second. It was a good thing he didn't eat that extra brownie at lunch because I leapt on him as though he was a bounce house. The little pond was approaching fast and suddenly, I realized a wooden sled plus a big brother weigh more than simply one little brother tippy toeing across semi frozen ice. A Christmas tree slightly slowed us down as it dumped a bucket full of snow from its branches on our faces upon impact. The scattered pine cones kept us from full throttle across the pond and we came to a screeching halt at the outer edge.

Grandma made us take our wet clothes off after entering the basement door. Our boots were soaked and she reminded us that only Jesus could walk across water. I told my brother we would inform our cousin, Phil, we made it to the water too and that wouldn't really be lying…unless the little engineer could figure out what wood submerged in pond water looked like.

The Christmas Tree Tractor

    Grandpa fired up the old Farmal tractor the Friday after Thanksgiving in hot pursuit of the Stump family Christmas tree. On the seventh turn of the ignition, the exhaust roared out of the top pipe usually covered with a coffee can. He raised the old boom bucket hungry for pine branches. It looked like a monster's mouth drooling for just a taste of sap. I told my little brother, who Grandpa called Tad-poll, the metal jaws would eat him if he wasn't careful. I was jealous that he got to ride along on Grandpa's lap to go get our Christmas tree without me.
    My dad would ride ski style from the hitch holding on to the duct-taped seatback for dear life. He was not the most athletic person you'd ever meet; scorekeeper for the Juniata J.V. basketball team back in his day. He was not exactly the kind of guy who could drive tractors or cut down trees. Dad wore a black Russian style furry hat that was truly embarrassing to me, especially when he walked us to the school bus stop in the snow. Grandpa was crowned King wearing one just like it for this time of year, except it was blaze orange. Tad was bundled up so you couldn't see his skin, wrapped in hand me downs, moon boots, with a hood tied so tight his chin would get a rash.
    Three generations of Stumps headed up the hill to cut the perfect tree down to its stump roots. Grandpa saw this as the perfect opportunity to save a penny and allow more funds for home heating oil, outdoor ornaments, peanut butter brittle and electricity.
    "It would be absolutely ridiculous to spend hard earned cash on a ragged old tree weed in town that hadn't been watered in weeks. Besides that is a god awful excuse for laziness. You might as well throw your money out the window at Old Man Winter."
    The trees dotted the farm field hill here and there in no order at all. White pines and a few Douglas Firs for the family sprouted out

completely un-pruned. Grandpa Stump had a theory that if the trees were aligned in a row they'd suck up each other's soil nutrients. It would also appear to the neighbors that you cared too much. You don't want them to think you have too much time to waste.

Sitting shotgun on the one seater tractor, Tad's five year old animation broke through Grandpa's puffy parka and nudged a little at his frozen heart. Grandpa let him hold the steering wheel.

"Straight ahead sailor! No, you can't play with the bucket Sonny!" Grandpa didn't say much else but watched his little grandson hold tight to the rubber wheel with all he had and pretended not to notice.

When they mounted the summit of Stump's hill, a slight squabble broke out between second and third generation over which tree was right for the pick'in. Tad ran around a giant towering green, but Dad insisted it wouldn't fit snug on top of the woody wagon. You know your family drives the 'humiliation mobile' when your tree held down with bungee chords matches the wood grain siding perfectly. Grandpa pleaded the fifth, sitting there with a saw sharpener he dug up out of the workshop. He had brought the file along, just in case, and was gliding it across his fingernails.

Dad stood there giving little Tad a version of his own theory over how to reduce pine needle droppings by cutting the base at a certain angle.

"Seventy eight degrees should do now son." Grandpa dismounted his tractor saddle growing impatient at the uneven saw strokes of his grandson.

"Here!" he said and took over with carpenter's hands. Tad danced like a little Indian around the tree, high on pine while Grandpa whacked away at the wood. Sap trickled down over the saw in slow motion and suddenly the tree listed leeward.

"Timber!" yelled the younger sons in unison. Grandpa just shook his head and grunted.

They fed her to the monster's mouth and headed down over the hill bumping all the way. They left one more stump to landscape Old Stump's farm hill. A simple thought floated through Grandpa's furry cap. No artificial tree could take the place of this Christmas memory.

"No Siree!"

The Antenna Star

Grandma told me all the neighbors were making a fuss wondering if the old star was going to guide them over Mifflin Hill during the Christmas season. As Grandpa Stump's strength diminished with the seasons of life, so too did the star's altitude on the old TV antenna tower. Years before the tower was the conduit for Channel Eight and Channel Ten reception, an incredible two channel choice instead of only one. Grandpa would climb on up the antenna annually, about the time you'd start to see your breath smoke. He would hoist up the hand crafted star made out of one by planks and old fashioned C9-1/4 Christmas bulbs.

I remember when I was little, Grandma told me not to stare too long at the star, or I'd go cross eyed like Great Uncle Pete. That was scary, because Old Pete had a glass eyeball from the war and would take it out and wink at me. Now Grandma was strongly suggesting I should get the star on the right rung and make sure the bulbs were working correctly. I'd have to climb twenty five feet and be eye to eye with the flashing widow-maker. Seems her concern for her grandson's personal safety was fading.

Grandpa had kept his safe distance from the passerby's after plugging the orange chord into the light socket.

He watched neighbors braking and children gawking from inside the window and muttered, "This show case is costing me way too much electricity. If one goes out they all go out!" He kept the star on a timer.

Grandpa and Grandma had their unique style for decorating. Grandpa placed two noel candles, one a little higher than the other(hence the discount at Big Lots) on the cement steps. There was a blue light bulb for the porch instead of the regular yellow. Grandma unwrapped newspaper from the Star of David, which looked more like the star of his grandson, Abijah. She exhaled into one inflatable Christmas ball and passed it out the storm door for Grandpa to hang with a wooden clothespin from the sagging clothes line. Grandma instructed Grandpa to place one brown matchstick wreath that appeared to have taken on a forest fire, over the porch window. He pretended stapling the orange utility cord to the wayne's coat ceiling was more of a priority. Grandma loved an overdose of décor more and more. Grandpa enjoyed less and less, the chore of exterior design each year.

    I pulled the brittle star out of retirement the year Grandpa went to celebrate Jesus Birthday at His home in Heaven. It was covered in cobwebs out in the garage port and saturated by dust. I used my own fingers to feel the delicate dip painted bulbs Grandpa used to bring to life. The whole thing was wrapped in tin foil to give it the extra flare of fakeness. He believed this gave adequate combustible protection in case it caught fire due to electrical engineering miscalculations, like the fifty four staples driven through the plastic braided green wire.

    Amazingly, the lights still worked. Grandpa's hunk of handmade Christmas guided me home to see Grandma that Christmas Eve, to give her the company he could no longer provide. Walking around my red Geo Storm with an oozing glow on the hood I paused in the ice covered lane. I looked way, way up to the top of his antenna and was entranced by the guiding light that hovered over the old brick farm house. I knew then how the Wisemen felt to finally be at His home. I fidgeted under the star like a little kid high on candy canes debating weather to go inside or savor the moment. I was home for the holidays under the warming glow of the old antenna star.

Heading into Town

Grandpa took Grandma out to McDonald's on Monday evenings. The Senior Citizen specials could not be beat by an old cheapskate. He saved gas mileage with his baby blue, gently used Cadillac by parking in the handicapped spot. But he spent those savings on hot fudge sundaes, loaded with nuts and extra fudge. Grandma liked the seats at McDonald's better than Reed's Diner. She said you could feel another person's arse pushing through the cushions at Reed's. And she wouldn't let a stranger poke an arse into her backside. Grandpa wouldn't tolerate it either, because he'd hear about it the whole way home.

The elderly couple had to be there at precisely 4:50. Ten minutes till five in order to beat the small town crowd driving home from Harrisburg and the local lumber yards. You wouldn't think there was much of a rush hour living in a town with 861 people and one Sherriff, who sat at the Mifflin Hill curve trying to cash in on the meager number of fast food drivers. But Grandpa and Grandma were there at 4:50 none the less.

Grandma wanted to guarantee she'd get a fresher bun and enjoy free refills she insisted would expire when it got dark outside. She would stick extra napkins in her purse for home along with ketchup, salt packets, coffee creamers and straws. She figured Ronald was doing well enough since she kept seeing his commercials on primetime TV.

Grandpa liked to see his favorite high school girl behind the counter at 5:00. He would give her a nickel or dime tip depending on how much she amused him. He insisted on giving the coins to her instead of the children's hospital, but told her not to get any piercings with her earnings, or she'd end up there. One time he gave her a coupon for a free order of french fries over at the burger king. She looked at him like the transaction was illegal, and he winked back at her flirtatiously.

Grandma required extra time at the cash register digging for coupons. She had kept every single one that came in the Sunday paper in the last five years. They were held together by a paper clip in her purse, and she had to find the right stack of unexpired Big and Tasty bucks. She squabbled with the poor cashier if the date was up, and said the print was so fine they must make exceptions for senior citizens with bi-focals.

"Not as fine as you though darling," Grandpa added, while winking at the cashier. Grandma reared her head and giggled thinking the silly comment was aimed to flatter her, while the cashier rolled her eyes and checked the clock to see how much time was left in her five hour shift.

They sat in a booth out of the sun's glare to the west yet as close to the blowing heater over the drafty door as they could stand. They liked to look for people they knew but pretended not to notice them. Grandma would spot someone from the church kitchen out of the corner of her eye and inform Stump with an entire romance novel about them before they passed by and exchanged pleasant hellos. Grandpa would look out the window at the new Chevrolets and dream about pulling up the drive through lane putting down the electric window and sweet talking the young gal in the speaker.

They would take the long way home through Mifflintown. Grandpa secretly loved to inspect how the houses he had built on the outskirts of town as side jobs were still standing. The white one behind the diner with southern plantation piers was his favorite. Grandma complained about all the changes downtown. Her favorite shoe store had closed after they opened the Wal-Mart up in Lewistown. She was still putting tape around her zip up boots instead of giving in and buying a replacement brand. The Methodist church had a new minister who did not visit enough according to her liking. And she could not get comfortable with all the foreigners on the sidewalks who were all working at the chicken plant. She'd watch the news late at night and ask Stump if the flood light was on and the doors were locked tight.

Just over the railroad bridge, they would finally turn right on Licking Creek Road. Driving past the Citgo station with the blinking yellow light meant the Sheriff was on duty. The old distributer without a Visa sticker in the window and the 'Welcome Hunters' Yuengling sign still buzzed 'Open' with neon. Up along Mifflin Hill they could see the tunnel steps coming up from the railroad bed. Grandpa thought about how Charlie's boys would try to beat his car on foot across that old graffitied underground shortcut. He would pass by June's Bait Shop up on the alley and Grandma would wave at someone sitting on their porch. They would roll down around the S-curve and breeze by the horse farm Charlie always talked about buying as a boy. There was the mill with junk scattered all over, strewn every which way in no apparent order. Grandma would lean forward in her seat to look at the houses in Stump's Development, wondering what her oldest son was fiddling with out in his garage.

They would both peer up to the new wooden house with the paved lane Grandpa sold the land rights to in order to have pocket money for a little while longer. Every light was on in the peak windows, and they obviously did not believe in being stingy with electricity. Finally, down over the hill, they were approaching their house at last. They'd stop and lean out the window to check the mail at the bottom of the lane, but it was only bills and prescription meds. Grandpa would k turn the Cadillac in the stones and let Grandma off at the broken cement pavers. He'd sit inside the car listening to the radio for one last tune as she slowly worked her way to the porch steps.

A Loretta Lynn song fizzled over the a.m. radio. He mouthed the lyrics with no audible sound but his wheezy breathing as the familiar tune buzzed in his head and heart.

The work we done was hard at night, we'd sleep cause we were tired
I never thought of leavin Butcher Holler, but lots of things have changed since the way back then
And it's so good to be back home again
Not much left but the floor, nothing lives there anymore
Just the mem'ries of a coal miner's daughter.

He thought about his years at the farm trying to make ends meet with dairy cows and a welding job up at the steel mill. He was thankful the cows were all gone but, admittedly, he missed the smells, the coolness of the barn and the rush of repairs. He coughed a deep raspy cough at the flashback of all those years of hard work, spilled milk, sawdust, metal shavings and sweat. The living room window light clicked on, and he pondered how quiet the old brick farmhouse was with all the children grown and gone. He sat alone in his old blue Cadillac, engine still running and radio crackling, drifting him away as darkness crept in over the farmstead. He felt a chill and turned up the thermostat on the Cadillac console. But something inside him was cold as midnight and he could not get warm. He turned the key to the off position, completed the chore of getting out of the car and stiffly staggered to the steps.

Hospital Visits and Kit Kats

Thad and I met at Weis supermarket to pick up kit kats. Grandpa was addicted to them. I knew he wouldn't be allowed to eat them in the hospital, but we snuck them in anyway. I brought along a copy of *Tuesday's with Morrie*. I had opened up the chapter called regrets and highlighted, "Forgive yourself then forgive others." I wrote down a few words on the opening page. I told him the book reminded me of him. I said there was always something powerful that pulled me off his exit on the highway home. I never stopped at the farm because I felt obligated, but because I wanted to. I signed off as Nat instead of Nate. I hated when he called me Nat, but that was his way of expressing affection to me.

On the elevator ride up to the fourth floor, Thad and I talked about how Grandpa had tried to break out of the nursing home a few weeks before. He asked Tad to wheel him down the hallway of Locust Grove and slip out the side door. He told Tad he simply had to get back to the farm and see Dottie. He added that he always wanted to take a ride in a foreign car to point out all the shortcomings to my brother personally, so he'd see American made metal was king. They were putting his flannel shirt on over his pajamas when our parents walked in the room and put an end to the discussion all together. Grandpa ended up slapping my mom in the face over the whole thing and Thad said he had never seen our father so fuming mad. Grandpa did get out of the nursing home, but rode in an ambulance instead of a Honda Accord.

I had his hospital room number scribbled down on a pink slip. I had called Grandma back at the farm house two hours prior and found out he was still in room 410. We walked right by the nurses station scanning numbers. The place smelled of commercial tile, medicine, bleach and old people all mixed together. We walked inside the dark room and walked right back out.

There was an old, shriveled up man lying on the chair in there. He had tubes tied to him, dripping bags holding fluids overhead, and was fast asleep.

Thad even said out loud, "That's not Grandpa!"

We didn't want to disturb the frozen looking stranger, so we slipped back out to the nurses station.

"Do you know what room John Stump Sr. is in?"

"Yes, room 410."

"Well that's funny because I know what my grandfather looks like and that's not him in 410," I said.

"Yes it is sir," she replied.

She escorted us back into the room and went to the old man's bedside. I felt so awkward standing there tapping with impatience as she started to question the incapacitated human.

"John, wake up John. John, do you know these boys?" His eyes squinted in the glimmer of sunlight streaming into the dark room. His voice began to search for strength and he coughed out the words

"Sure that's Tad and Nat. They're Charlie's boys, good boys."

I wanted to fall down on the floor in a fetal position and cry. It was him, Grandpa Stump. He was so unrecognizable with all the hospital equipment enveloping him in the aftermath of cancer surgery, his own grandsons could not see him for who he was.

I could barely say the words, "I'm sorry," to the nurse and to him, but she seemed to understand, like she was used to this type of uncomfortable interaction.

I walked over to his bed staring at his sunken face, toothless grin and rough shaven wrinkles that were starting to stretch.

"We brought you some kit kats, Grandpa," I said with tears streaming down my humiliated face.

Thad took out the ten pack of kit kats and Grandpa's expression lit up like a little kid in the checkout counter line.

"Can I have them all?" he asked.

I opened up a pack and held it to his lips. He started chewing with delight, and Thad and I had to laugh. The chocolate started to smear up on his chin like a toddler eating m&m's for the first time. His dentures were out and we had never seen him without his fake smile.

"Can I have another?" he asked before the first was finished.

Just then a second shift nurse walked in to take his blood pressure. He looked up at her with a mischievous smile and chewed loudly. We opened up another and he savored every bite while she did her routine and tried not to make eye contact.

"This place isn't very exciting," Grandpa said. "In fact this is the most exciting thing that's happened all week, boys!"

We tried to carry on a conversation like normal but soon ran out of things worthwhile to mention. A feeling deep inside told me this would be our last conversation so make every word count. I showed him the book but he did not seem interested in a book.

I asked him if he'd been reading the paper and he said, "No sense!"

Just then more of our family members started coming through the door.

I'll never forget how his face lit up and he scooted up a bit in his chair when Grandma hobbled into the room. She gave him a flirtatious homecoming queen wave and told him she'd give him a kiss but didn't want him to catch this virus going around. I sat right beside him on the bed watching. Soon everyone's bantering conversations took over the room. Laurie was sitting on the floor talking about her headache from the night before. Buster sat on the porta pot telling exaggerated salmon fishing stories. Our Dad and Aunt Mary Kay were discussing medical insurance and Thad had stepped out to check out a gorgeous nurse that just floated by with a medicine cart. I sat studying my Grandfather. His rough workman's hands had built our entire family. His farmer flannel shirt smelled like the cramped living room at the farmhouse. His cowlick was flipped like a rooster's and he didn't bother wetting it down. Grandpa was growing uncomfortable with so many people around.

"I want to go to sleep," he said, and the room fell silent.

One by one the Stump family trickled out giving him a hug, a kiss, or a Hallmark card quote. I sat by him and savored the last seconds. When I was left all alone with Grandpa, I bent down and kissed him on the forehead, partially because it felt right but also because he couldn't stop me at this point in his life. He had never been an affectionate man.

He asked me where Mare was and I said, "She really likes you Grandpa, for some reason she really likes you."

He told me to tell her that he liked her too, and that we would do good together.

"You already know that don't you?"

"Yes I do Grandpa, I know."

I told him I loved him and he said, "I love you, too, but that Tad, Tad's my buddy."

I said, "I know, but I will have to tackle him when I get outside and tell him Grandpa likes him better."

"No, no, you're a good boy too Nat, you're good boys." He closed his eyes and drifted off to sleep.

Thad and I were his pall bearers. His cherry wood coffin was heavier than we were prepared for. I told Thad and our cousins struggling to lift the wood into the hearse, we shouldn't have put so many kit kats in his hand before they closed the casket. We buried him on the Mifflin hillside that looks out over Grandpa's ridge. The extended Stump family all went back to the farm that afternoon and ate spaghetti on the porch. We played a rowdy game of football in the barnyard and Little Phil ran right into one of those Rose of Sharon trees Grandpa had planted and replanted for Grandma. You should have heard her yell at us, shaking her cane in the air from the farm porch steps. Later, I dug it out and planted it along my stone driveway with a couple other shoots.

That evening right before sunset, I took my .22 and walked up on Grandpa's ridge. I traveled the old logging road and stopped at the second bend to look down over the farm. I pulled out a kit kat from my pocket and unwrapped the silver lining. As I took a bite, I tried to savor the farm in case it disappeared. I could see the pond glowing green where cows no longer came to quench their summer thirst. I peered down to the old red barn bleeding while blending in with the crayola colored leaves of the picture postcard hills. I could hear the grandchildren and great grandchildren's intonations fading while playing in the last deep breaths of sunset. I could vaguely make out the yellow lamp light in the front lawn that just clicked on with the old fashioned dial timer. I thought about how life is just a vapor and then it fades in fast forward. I wondered what would happen to Grandpa's farm.

Neighbors like Bummy

The first time I saw neighbor Bummy he was scaling the steep hill behind the farm, bailing hay with Grandpa's tractor and waving to me at the same time. Most people would have been afraid to take a four wheeler up the same hill, but not Bummy. He told me that one time it ran away on him coming down from the top, and he used the bucket to slow himself down. He had moved into Aunt Mary Kay's empty grey house when she headed south for vacation and never came back. He was the kind of neighbor that would come calling whenever and could fix whatever. Grandpa took an instant liking to him because he could repair anything and everything at the farm and didn't have to say much while working.

He was a skinny man who looked like ZZ Top with a long beard draping down to his belt, wearing a faded ball cap, tinted glasses, and perfect teeth when he smiled shyly. His garage wall could tell you a thousand stories while he bent over in silence on the concrete floor working on an old Cub Cadet mower, designing his own hydraulic log splitter, or adjusting the carburetor on his Harley. He could simply appear up on the ridge during hunting season, tell you about a massive 10 pointer someone had seen on a game camera, and then he would vanish like a ghost. Grandma was a little too chatty for him to be completely comfortable around her, but he always treated her with chivalry and respect when she'd yell for him from the porch. She had Bummy's number written at the top of the list on her TV tray and used it habitually.

He brought Grandma over a little grey kitten one spring after Grandpa had passed. He had his teenage daughter with him, who was carrying a couple of kittens in a cardboard box and let Grandma have first pick. Bummy had so many cats they would fall out of his garage rafters now and then. If I was hanging out over there catching up on neighborhood news, sipping on one of his fresh black and tans from the tap, I'd keep a nervous eye on the rafters for appearing cats. He'd spread a quarter bag of feed all at one time on the floor and let the critters have a buffet. He said the cats kept the pests away in the barns and garages, and his wife could simply not say no when someone dropped a litter off. Grandma ended up saying she didn't really want one, but set a bowl out on the porch and looked for the grey cat each morning anyway. Bummy would secretly bring it over on his tractor seat and gently drop it off behind the wagon-shed if Grandma started complaining that she hadn't seen it in a week. She said she was done having pets but I don't know who she fancied more, Bummy, or that cat.

Bummy put a lot of time in giving free neighborly help at the farm. He installed new water lines from the spring house two hundred yards down to the farmhouse. He even crawled deep into the cistern and cleaned it out when they found two squirrels floating inside. No wonder Grandma's ice tea didn't taste like perfection for a few weeks. He fixed the copper pipes in the basement and installed a new boiler after Grandpa couldn't chop wood with a maul anymore. He harvested the field corn, bailed the hay, and mowed the two acres of farmhouse yard with his own mower. He would fix Grandpa's tractor when everyone else said it was time to trade it in. He even bought the old Dodge Duster stored in the machine shed bay. Grandpa had purchased the used car as a tug boat for his baby blue vintage Caddy, but Bummy bought it and taught his oldest daughter how to drive and change the oil.

Bummy did not come to the church part of Grandpa's and eventually Grandma's funeral. But he was at the cemetery hill in a button down shirt and poorly tied tie looking out at the ridge. I barely recognized him without a hat. He showed me how you could see Grandpa's ridge from the grave plots and said it was the perfect place for them to rest side by side. He invited me over for a black and tan when things calmed down at the farmhouse. We didn't have to say a word hanging out in his cluttered garage. I looked around at his antique tools, his deer racks, his beefy orange and black motorcycle, and the snowshoes on his wall. They took my mind off the hard side of life for a while. He told me if I bought the place he'd help me fix it up. Run new electric lines that would be up to code, tap into public sewage and restore the glory. He showed me the plot map with the three acres Grandpa had basically given him just like the tractor for all his hard work. He pointed to the old courthouse farm survey and showed me how the plot resembled a church steeple. We joked over the fact that maybe that's why three of the family became ministers. He told me there was more land up there than the children think.

"I'd love to see you get this old farm," he said.

The Farm Pond

The spring after my grandfather passed away I took a stroll up to the old spring-fed pond. The water was Gatorade frost blue, mixed with the touch of a southern girl with green eyes. It sounded surreal and Caribbean. It reminded me of 'Freshy Pond', a small oasis in West End Bahamas where children leap from a rock ledge. The trickle of the spring piped water hitting the rock channel hypnotized me.

"I have to restore this surrounding to match its inner beauty," I thought, and fired up Grandpa's eager beaver chainsaw.

All around the pond, time had taken over. Prickers clawed their way up the banks. Weeds towered over my head. The diving board Uncle Buster had framed was rusted away, and the far bank was overrun with grape vines. The hoof prints of dairy cows our dog, Joy guarded as we fished for sunnies were long gone. The bank where I shot my BB gun at fish rising to feed in the summer sunset was blocked by an ugly split pine tree engulfed in thorns. The upper end, where farm boys brought buckets of bass to supply the new pond, was now impenetrable. I pulled the rope-start and began to fight what was now forgotten.

As I began to tear into that thicket hedge I wondered who else had forgotten their days at a farm pond; summer days when a black striped bass swallowed an entire sunny on the end of a bamboo pool line; winter afternoons with black and white skates, a hockey stick, or sled runway. Those days seemed so far away. You remember when little Richie fell off the rope swing because his brothers were flirting with their gals on a blanket just out of eyesight.

I can see my best friend Steve's ankle cracking through the ice because we told him, "Yes it is safe to walk over there!"

You hear the bullfrogs grunting for companionship and trace back a late night on the porch. You see the soda pop bubbles and recall how cringing, yet cool, it was to walk barefoot through the silky mud. Farm ponds were a lake to us as children. But, so soon, we forget the path to the hangout spot.

I poured gasoline on a thorn bush root and lit a hungry flame. As I watched the ground burn brown and the root go black it took me back. I recalled the fire my brother, Thaddeus, had with his girlfriend Jenna. The idea is, you throw on one less log so you can keep her warm.

I remember Grandma yelling at us from the back porch, "Put that damn fire out and get the hen inside."

I see my buddy Steve with his guitar playing one more we can all sing. I envision a cigarette sparkler foaming as it hits the water after being flicked. As the pile of the first man, Adam's cursed thorns and thistles crack in the rain, I swear they will not get a foothold at this farm pond.

Bummy, came up on Grandpa's old Farmal Tractor and plowed the remnants I had tugged by blood and sweat to the meadow. He always has an inside story and tells me some boys from down the road must have stolen some of the bigger fish in the pond. I smile as I picture them sneaking to Grandpa's pond with a five gallon, white hydraulic fluid bucket. *Let them be boys with farm pond stories of glory*, I think to myself. Bummy and I both confirmed that the old un-catchable carp, who must be twenty years old by now, is still stalking the nine foot deep end of the pond. Matter of fact, last time I snuck up on the weed wacked bank and stared deep into the dark green shelf, I swear I saw its shadow!

The Burning Barrel

Grandma kept a scrap bucket on the kitchen counter. It was full of egg shells, tea bags, mystery meat from the meals on wheels and many other stray cat snacks. She kept her trash in a supermarket paper bag which made lighting it on fire in the burning barrel a little easier.

If family came to visit she would give you a kiss goodbye from her weathered green rocking chair and say, "It sure would be nice if someone took the trash out to the barrel."

She never made a direct request, but it's not like she was going to hobble out there with her walker. Besides you would feel bad if you ever heard she cracked another hip and lay out there on the porch rug because her emergency necklace button didn't work right.

She wore a emergency communication device around her multi layered sweaters with style. Also around her neck was a big shiny emerald looking thing, something her daughter, Mary Kay, had ordered for her from QVC. The obnoxious jewel necklace could place a call to E.M.S. and only misfired once which resulted in a huge argument between Grandma and the operator. Grandma thought it was ridiculous that someone would call during her afternoon shows and the attendant couldn't hear well because Oprah was blaring on the console TV. She ended up sending an ambulance to RD3 and Grandma railed into the driver about not daring to send a bill for their own ill conceived practice drill.

We had quite a few bags to burn after my mother's 60th birthday party on the farm lawn. Grandma said it was the first grand party she had hosted but always thought it was the perfect setting for a bed and breakfast with horse riding trails. We put up a big white tent out on the hill. Dad brought in a Christian honkey tonk band featuring an 82 year old harmonica man. He was quite entertaining as he sat in his chair with a 'pickin' guitar and a headset harmonica. Grandma watched from the porch with an approving smile as they sang, "Won't you build me a cabin in the corner of glory land." We had fried chicken from Wal-Mart, potato salad overdose and warm rolls that were not as good as Grandma's. She was very outspoken about letting everyone know this last fact.

Grandma was dressed to the hilt. She wore white shoes, earrings Aunt Mary Kay had delivered Fed Ex from QVC, and a flowery white dress with a light white sweater. Even though it was August 4th Grandma was renowned for feeling drafts. She watched my two year old daughter attempt to play croquet in the course her grandfather, Charlie, created for the occasion. Granny laughed a dainty laugh as Danny and his buddy played badminton in the garden against sister Lori and Big Bill. She waved like she was in a parade when Bummy stopped in on his Harley. She was quite content with the fact that there was a porta-pot brought in, and she would not have to worry about her septic tank overflowing.

It was the last hug she gave me from her porch as we prepared to put our daughter in her car seat. I can smell her sweet tea breath mixed with medicine and the Ben Gay scent of her clothing. Grandma went to Geisinger hospital the very next day with a brain aneurysm and never returned to the farm. We carried her casket up to the Presbyterian Cemetery that looks out over the farm ridge from town. She was 89 and 11 months old. She had told me a few weeks before that she was of no use to anyone anymore, just a bother. I told Grandma I loved her stories, that no one else in the family could remember anymore and tell with sharp detail like she could. I loved her iced tea with six seeping tea bags and two squirts of lemon. I loved the farm that always seemed to be home. It was the last central spot for our family to gather and share stories new and old.

Cousin Adam and I were hired to clean up the place for Auction. We filled three dumpsters full of her attic and cellar collections. We were given full access to the attic where she had always told us Granny's ghost lingered. I was scared to death to even look at the latch when passing from the bathroom but it was an antique collector's paradise. Once you got past the bat droppings there were old trunks with vintage clothing, a baby carriage, baseball cards, and old stamps. We found Mason Jars and old bottles, World War II food stamp rations, and perfume bottles. She kept old calendars and women's magazines piled higher than the light string.

FADING AMERICAN FARM

All of it only brought $3,000 at auction revealing that most of the stuff was glorified junk. Each of us as grandchildren and children were allowed to go through first and put a sticker on our three favorite things. I chose Grandpa's table saw from the workshop and his handmade wooden Christmas star. The sentimental star is hung behind my house at Christmas time. I use a deer climbing stand to shimmy up a birch tree for all the neighbors to see. From Grandma's 90 year collection of goodies, my wife selected an old painted milkjug.

We threw the burnable junk out the third floor window and picked it up with a wheelbarrow. Adam told me that mice poop was cancer causing and, therefore, was careful to keep his distance from the flames. The barrel all too quickly was an insufficient fire ring. So we took some old aluminum and a couple cement blocks and increased the perimeter. But Peep as Uncle Flip called him was always a bit of a pyro. One day, while I was picking up a sandwich at the Hoagie shop in town, Adam would of made Grandma pass out if she hadn't just gone to heaven some weeks before. He threw an old sofa from the garage on the burning pile and doused it with 87 octane. The sofa, along with a hundred Redbook magazines and six trash bags full of old Sentinel newspapers, made quite the kindling. The flames raced down the bank towards the garden, consuming October leaves with a menacing appetite.

Aunt Mary Kay ran for her cell phone to call the fire station and started yelling out loud whether she should press send or not. My dad, Charlie, who was on the porch with Uncle Buster discussing power of attorney and land surveys, broke for the hose but it would not reach past the garden fence even when he prayed out loud. Buster ran like hell for the first time in two decades to protect his inheritance. He yelled at Adam to work with him to rake the damn leaves from the fire's path. Adam ran over the coals with his Adidas Sambas and matching black pants and put a couple more holes in them both. He used a sickle to ram down the pricker bushes that would add fuel to the fire. The wind carried the smoke over the wagon-shed and high into the air for all the neighbors to panic over.

Bummy came running over to the farm from two houses down. Grandma would have called him semi-immediately from her rotary phone instead of the sheriff or volunteers who sat on lawnchairs outside the Fire Station garage door. Bummy had an extinguisher he kept in the back of his work truck and began to launch a cumulous cloud of gases over the burning bank. Charlie stood there squirting the green rubber hose from seventy five feet away, praying at embarrassingly loud decibels with his preacher voice. Buster raked a leaf onto his high athletic socks with the red stripe at the top and started dancing when a live red stripe ember started showing up on his ankle. Meanwhile, Adam, seeing that the flames were coming under control stopped to light up a cigarette with Grandpa's old barbecue lighter. Good old Bummy gave three final huffs from the red canister and stood on the hill, silently staring at Adam in amazement.

A Thursday Sentinel floated up from the simmering barrel and landed in my father's pointless spray pattern. Aunt Mary Kay, still holding her cell phone in the air and nervously pacing in the garden, reached down and picked the egg white clipping up. She ran over to Buster and Charlie who were now shaking hands with Bummy while glaring in disbelief at cousin Adam. Mary Kay held in her hand Dorothy Stump's obituary article. It was charred at one end and had been singed by the fire. The obituary was right next to an ad for the Ag Feedstore. Whispering words, mostly legible, but leaving certain blanks for the family to fill in met their watering eyes.

…"God saw you getting tired and a cure was not to be, so He put his arms around you and whispered, 'Come to me.' With tearful eyes we watched you and saw you pass away. Although we loved you dearly we could not make you stay. A golden heart stopped beating, hard working hands at rest. God broke our hearts to prove to us, he only takes the best"…

Grandpa's carpenter hands built everything on that farm to get our family started. And Grandma's golden heart kept us together, for better or worse. The farm still stands on Licking Creek Road with aged acres touched by time in every way. The silo has been torn down and the eves repainted in white. The lane needs repaved and the barn is fading from red to ocean wood grey. You can peek through spider web windows and see the restoration slowly taking place. But the fading porch light is always on and Grandma's stories linger still. I picture them both sitting on the old swing holding hands, watching for us to all come home.